	TRIP # _____
🗺️	FROM / TO
🗺️	ROUTE
⊘	MILEAGE

	WEATHER CONDIT
🌡️	_____ ☀️ ⛅
🚩	_____ ☐ ☐
📅	DATE

CAMPGROUND

NAME		LOCATION	☆☆☆☆☆
ADDRESS		SHOWERS	☆☆☆☆☆
PHONE		CAMPSTORE	☆☆☆☆☆
WEBSITE		LAUNDRY	☆☆☆☆☆
SITE #		WATER PRESSURE	☆☆☆☆☆
PRICE		OVERALL RATING	☆☆☆☆☆

HIGHLIGHTS

PLACES & ACTIVITIES

DINING & RESTAURANTS

Notes

	TRIP # _____
🗺️	FROM / TO
🗺️	ROUTE
🧭	MILEAGE

WEATHER CONDITIONS						
🌡️ _____	☀️	⛅	🌦️	🌧️	❄️
🚩 _____	☐	☐	☐	☐	☐
📅 DATE						

CAMPGROUND

	NAME		LOCATION	☆☆☆☆☆
📍	ADDRESS	🚿	SHOWERS	☆☆☆☆☆
📞	PHONE	🏪	CAMPSTORE	☆☆☆☆☆
🌐	WEBSITE	👕	LAUNDRY	☆☆☆☆☆
	SITE #	🚰	WATER PRESSURE	☆☆☆☆☆
💵	PRICE	⭐	OVERALL RATING	☆☆☆☆☆

HIGHLIGHTS

PLACES & ACTIVITIES

DINING & RESTAURANTS

Notes

TRIP # _____

- 🧭 FROM / TO
- 🗺️ ROUTE
- ⏱️ MILEAGE

WEATHER CONDITIONS

🌡️ _____ ☀️ ⛅ 🌧️ ⛈️ ❄️
🚩 _____ ☐ ☐ ☐ ☐ ☐

📅 DATE

CAMPGROUND

🏕️ NAME		🏞️ LOCATION	☆☆☆☆☆
📍 ADDRESS		🚿 SHOWERS	☆☆☆☆☆
📞 PHONE		🏪 CAMPSTORE	☆☆☆☆☆
🌐 WEBSITE		👕 LAUNDRY	☆☆☆☆☆
⛺ SITE #		🚰 WATER PRESSURE	☆☆☆☆☆
💵 PRICE		🤲 OVERALL RATING	☆☆☆☆☆

HIGHLIGHTS

PLACES & ACTIVITIES

DINING & RESTAURANTS

Notes

TRIP # _____

- FROM / TO
- ROUTE
- MILEAGE

WEATHER CONDITIONS

- 🌡 _____
- 🚩 _____
- DATE

CAMPGROUND

NAME	LOCATION ☆☆☆☆☆
ADDRESS	SHOWERS ☆☆☆☆☆
PHONE	CAMPSTORE ☆☆☆☆☆
WEBSITE	LAUNDRY ☆☆☆☆☆
SITE #	WATER PRESSURE ☆☆☆☆☆
PRICE	OVERALL RATING ☆☆☆☆☆

HIGHLIGHTS

PLACES & ACTIVITIES

DINING & RESTAURANTS

Notes

TRIP # _____

- FROM / TO
- ROUTE
- MILEAGE

WEATHER CONDITIONS

- Temperature: _____
- Wind: _____
- DATE

CAMPGROUND

NAME	LOCATION ☆☆☆☆☆
ADDRESS	SHOWERS ☆☆☆☆☆
PHONE	CAMPSTORE ☆☆☆☆☆
WEBSITE	LAUNDRY ☆☆☆☆☆
SITE #	WATER PRESSURE ☆☆☆☆☆
PRICE	OVERALL RATING ☆☆☆☆☆

HIGHLIGHTS

PLACES & ACTIVITIES

DINING & RESTAURANTS

Notes

	TRIP # _____
🗺️	FROM / TO
🗺️	ROUTE
⭕	MILEAGE

	WEATHER CONDITIONS	
🌡️	_____	☀️ ⛅ 🌧️ ⛈️ ❄️
🚩	_____	☐ ☐ ☐ ☐ ☐
📅	DATE	

CAMPGROUND

NAME		LOCATION	☆☆☆☆☆
ADDRESS		SHOWERS	☆☆☆☆☆
PHONE		CAMPSTORE	☆☆☆☆☆
WEBSITE		LAUNDRY	☆☆☆☆☆
SITE #		WATER PRESSURE	☆☆☆☆☆
PRICE		OVERALL RATING	☆☆☆☆☆

HIGHLIGHTS

PLACES & ACTIVITIES	DINING & RESTAURANTS

Notes

TRIP # _____

- FROM / TO
- ROUTE
- MILEAGE

WEATHER CONDITIONS

☀️ ⛅ 🌧️ ⛈️ ❄️

☐ ☐ ☐ ☐ ☐

- DATE

CAMPGROUND

NAME	LOCATION	☆☆☆☆☆
ADDRESS	SHOWERS	☆☆☆☆☆
PHONE	CAMPSTORE	☆☆☆☆☆
WEBSITE	LAUNDRY	☆☆☆☆☆
SITE #	WATER PRESSURE	☆☆☆☆☆
PRICE	OVERALL RATING	☆☆☆☆☆

HIGHLIGHTS

PLACES & ACTIVITIES

DINING & RESTAURANTS

Notes

	TRIP # _____
🗺️	FROM / TO
🗺️	ROUTE
🧭	MILEAGE

WEATHER CONDITIONS						
🌡️ _____	☀️	⛅	🌧️	⛈️	❄️
🚩 _____	☐	☐	☐	☐	☐
📅 DATE						

CAMPGROUND

NAME		LOCATION	☆☆☆☆☆
ADDRESS		SHOWERS	☆☆☆☆☆
PHONE		CAMPSTORE	☆☆☆☆☆
WEBSITE		LAUNDRY	☆☆☆☆☆
SITE #		WATER PRESSURE	☆☆☆☆☆
PRICE		OVERALL RATING	☆☆☆☆☆

HIGHLIGHTS

PLACES & ACTIVITIES

DINING & RESTAURANTS

Notes

TRIP # _____

- FROM / TO
- ROUTE
- MILEAGE

WEATHER CONDITIONS

☀️ ⛅ 🌧️ ⛈️ ❄️
☐ ☐ ☐ ☐ ☐

DATE

CAMPGROUND

NAME	LOCATION	☆☆☆☆☆
ADDRESS	SHOWERS	☆☆☆☆☆
PHONE	CAMPSTORE	☆☆☆☆☆
WEBSITE	LAUNDRY	☆☆☆☆☆
SITE #	WATER PRESSURE	☆☆☆☆☆
PRICE	OVERALL RATING	☆☆☆☆☆

HIGHLIGHTS

PLACES & ACTIVITIES

DINING & RESTAURANTS

Notes

TRIP # _____

- FROM / TO
- ROUTE
- MILEAGE

WEATHER CONDITIONS

🌡 _____   ☀ ⛅ 🌧 ⛈ ❄

🚩 _____   ☐ ☐ ☐ ☐ ☐

📅 DATE

CAMPGROUND

NAME	LOCATION ☆☆☆☆☆
ADDRESS	SHOWERS ☆☆☆☆☆
PHONE	CAMPSTORE ☆☆☆☆☆
WEBSITE	LAUNDRY ☆☆☆☆☆
SITE #	WATER PRESSURE ☆☆☆☆☆
PRICE	OVERALL RATING ☆☆☆☆☆

HIGHLIGHTS

PLACES & ACTIVITIES

DINING & RESTAURANTS

Notes

TRIP # _____

- FROM / TO
- ROUTE
- MILEAGE

WEATHER CONDITIONS

- 🌡 _____ ☀ ⛅ 🌧 ⛈ ❄
- 🚩 _____ ☐ ☐ ☐ ☐ ☐
- 📅 DATE

CAMPGROUND

NAME	LOCATION	☆☆☆☆☆
ADDRESS	SHOWERS	☆☆☆☆☆
PHONE	CAMPSTORE	☆☆☆☆☆
WEBSITE	LAUNDRY	☆☆☆☆☆
SITE #	WATER PRESSURE	☆☆☆☆☆
PRICE	OVERALL RATING	☆☆☆☆☆

HIGHLIGHTS

PLACES & ACTIVITIES

DINING & RESTAURANTS

Notes

TRIP # _____	**WEATHER CONDITIONS**
FROM / TO	🌡 ____ ☀ ⛅ 🌧 ⛈ ❄
ROUTE	🚩 ____ ☐ ☐ ☐ ☐ ☐
MILEAGE	DATE

CAMPGROUND

NAME	LOCATION	☆☆☆☆☆
ADDRESS	SHOWERS	☆☆☆☆☆
PHONE	CAMPSTORE	☆☆☆☆☆
WEBSITE	LAUNDRY	☆☆☆☆☆
SITE #	WATER PRESSURE	☆☆☆☆☆
PRICE	OVERALL RATING	☆☆☆☆☆

HIGHLIGHTS

PLACES & ACTIVITIES

DINING & RESTAURANTS

Notes

	TRIP # _____
FROM / TO	
ROUTE	
MILEAGE	

WEATHER CONDITIONS						
🌡 _____	☀	⛅	🌧	⛈	❄
🚩 _____	☐	☐	☐	☐	☐
📅 DATE						

CAMPGROUND

NAME		LOCATION	☆☆☆☆☆
ADDRESS		SHOWERS	☆☆☆☆☆
PHONE		CAMPSTORE	☆☆☆☆☆
WEBSITE		LAUNDRY	☆☆☆☆☆
SITE #		WATER PRESSURE	☆☆☆☆☆
PRICE		OVERALL RATING	☆☆☆☆☆

HIGHLIGHTS

PLACES & ACTIVITIES

DINING & RESTAURANTS

Notes

TRIP # _____		WEATHER CONDITIONS	
FROM / TO		🌡 ____ ☀ ⛅ 🌧 ⛈ ❄	
ROUTE		🚩 ____ ☐ ☐ ☐ ☐ ☐	
MILEAGE		DATE	

CAMPGROUND

NAME		LOCATION	☆☆☆☆☆
ADDRESS		SHOWERS	☆☆☆☆☆
PHONE		CAMPSTORE	☆☆☆☆☆
WEBSITE		LAUNDRY	☆☆☆☆☆
SITE #		WATER PRESSURE	☆☆☆☆☆
PRICE		OVERALL RATING	☆☆☆☆☆

HIGHLIGHTS

PLACES & ACTIVITIES

DINING & RESTAURANTS

Notes

	TRIP # _____
🗺	FROM / TO
🗺	ROUTE
🚗	MILEAGE

WEATHER CONDITIONS						
🌡 _____	☀	⛅	🌧	⛈	❄
🚩 _____	☐	☐	☐	☐	☐
📅 DATE						

CAMPGROUND

🏕 NAME		🏞 LOCATION		☆☆☆☆☆
📍 ADDRESS		🚿 SHOWERS		☆☆☆☆☆
📞 PHONE		🏪 CAMPSTORE		☆☆☆☆☆
🌐 WEBSITE		👕 LAUNDRY		☆☆☆☆☆
⛺ SITE #		🚰 WATER PRESSURE		☆☆☆☆☆
💵 PRICE		⭐ OVERALL RATING		☆☆☆☆☆

HIGHLIGHTS

PLACES & ACTIVITIES

DINING & RESTAURANTS

Notes

TRIP # _____

- FROM / TO
- ROUTE
- MILEAGE

WEATHER CONDITIONS

🌡 _____ ☀️ ⛅ 🌧 ⛈ ❄️

🚩 _____ ☐ ☐ ☐ ☐ ☐

📅 DATE

CAMPGROUND

NAME	LOCATION	☆☆☆☆☆
ADDRESS	SHOWERS	☆☆☆☆☆
PHONE	CAMPSTORE	☆☆☆☆☆
WEBSITE	LAUNDRY	☆☆☆☆☆
SITE #	WATER PRESSURE	☆☆☆☆☆
PRICE	OVERALL RATING	☆☆☆☆☆

HIGHLIGHTS

PLACES & ACTIVITIES

DINING & RESTAURANTS

Notes

TRIP # _____

- FROM / TO
- ROUTE
- MILEAGE

WEATHER CONDITIONS

🌡 _____ ☀ ⛅ 🌧 ⛈ ❄
🚩 _____ ☐ ☐ ☐ ☐ ☐

📅 DATE

CAMPGROUND

NAME		LOCATION	☆☆☆☆☆
ADDRESS		SHOWERS	☆☆☆☆☆
PHONE		CAMPSTORE	☆☆☆☆☆
WEBSITE		LAUNDRY	☆☆☆☆☆
SITE #		WATER PRESSURE	☆☆☆☆☆
PRICE		OVERALL RATING	☆☆☆☆☆

HIGHLIGHTS

PLACES & ACTIVITIES

DINING & RESTAURANTS

Notes

TRIP # _____

- FROM / TO
- ROUTE
- MILEAGE

WEATHER CONDITIONS

- 🌡 _____ ☀️ ⛅ 🌧 ⛈ ❄️
- 🚩 _____ ☐ ☐ ☐ ☐ ☐
- 📅 DATE

CAMPGROUND

NAME	LOCATION	☆☆☆☆☆
ADDRESS	SHOWERS	☆☆☆☆☆
PHONE	CAMPSTORE	☆☆☆☆☆
WEBSITE	LAUNDRY	☆☆☆☆☆
SITE #	WATER PRESSURE	☆☆☆☆☆
PRICE	OVERALL RATING	☆☆☆☆☆

HIGHLIGHTS

PLACES & ACTIVITIES

DINING & RESTAURANTS

Notes

	TRIP # _____
🚩	FROM / TO
🗺️	ROUTE
🧭	MILEAGE

WEATHER CONDITIONS						
🌡️ _____	☀️	⛅	🌧️	⛈️	❄️
🚩 _____	☐	☐	☐	☐	☐
📅 DATE					

CAMPGROUND

🏕️ NAME		🏞️ LOCATION		☆☆☆☆☆
📍 ADDRESS		🚿 SHOWERS		☆☆☆☆☆
📞 PHONE		🏪 CAMPSTORE		☆☆☆☆☆
🌐 WEBSITE		👕 LAUNDRY		☆☆☆☆☆
⛺ SITE #		🚰 WATER PRESSURE		☆☆☆☆☆
💵 PRICE		🤲 OVERALL RATING		☆☆☆☆☆

HIGHLIGHTS

_____
_____
_____
_____
_____

PLACES & ACTIVITIES	DINING & RESTAURANTS

Notes

TRIP # _____

- FROM / TO
- ROUTE
- MILEAGE

WEATHER CONDITIONS

🌡 _____ ☀️ ⛅ 🌦 ⛈ ❄️

🚩 _____ ☐ ☐ ☐ ☐ ☐

📅 DATE

CAMPGROUND

NAME	LOCATION	☆☆☆☆☆
ADDRESS	SHOWERS	☆☆☆☆☆
PHONE	CAMPSTORE	☆☆☆☆☆
WEBSITE	LAUNDRY	☆☆☆☆☆
SITE #	WATER PRESSURE	☆☆☆☆☆
PRICE	OVERALL RATING	☆☆☆☆☆

HIGHLIGHTS

PLACES & ACTIVITIES

DINING & RESTAURANTS

Notes

TRIP # _____

- FROM / TO
- ROUTE
- MILEAGE

WEATHER CONDITIONS

- DATE

CAMPGROUND

NAME	LOCATION	☆☆☆☆☆
ADDRESS	SHOWERS	☆☆☆☆☆
PHONE	CAMPSTORE	☆☆☆☆☆
WEBSITE	LAUNDRY	☆☆☆☆☆
SITE #	WATER PRESSURE	☆☆☆☆☆
PRICE	OVERALL RATING	☆☆☆☆☆

HIGHLIGHTS

PLACES & ACTIVITIES

DINING & RESTAURANTS

Notes

TRIP # _____

- 🧭 FROM / TO
- 🗺️ ROUTE
- ⭕ MILEAGE

WEATHER CONDITIONS

🌡️ _____   ☀️ ⛅ 🌧️ ⛈️ ❄️

🚩 _____   ☐ ☐ ☐ ☐ ☐

📅 DATE

CAMPGROUND

🏕️ NAME	🌲 LOCATION	☆☆☆☆☆
📍 ADDRESS	🚿 SHOWERS	☆☆☆☆☆
📞 PHONE	🏪 CAMPSTORE	☆☆☆☆☆
🌐 WEBSITE	👕 LAUNDRY	☆☆☆☆☆
⛺ SITE #	🚰 WATER PRESSURE	☆☆☆☆☆
💵 PRICE	⭐ OVERALL RATING	☆☆☆☆☆

HIGHLIGHTS

PLACES & ACTIVITIES

DINING & RESTAURANTS

Notes

TRIP # _____

- 🧭 FROM / TO
- 🗺️ ROUTE
- ⚪ MILEAGE

WEATHER CONDITIONS

🌡️ _____ ☀️ ⛅ 🌦️ 🌧️ ❄️
🚩 _____ ☐ ☐ ☐ ☐ ☐

📅 DATE

CAMPGROUND

NAME		LOCATION	☆☆☆☆☆
ADDRESS		SHOWERS	☆☆☆☆☆
PHONE		CAMPSTORE	☆☆☆☆☆
WEBSITE		LAUNDRY	☆☆☆☆☆
SITE #		WATER PRESSURE	☆☆☆☆☆
PRICE		OVERALL RATING	☆☆☆☆☆

HIGHLIGHTS

PLACES & ACTIVITIES

DINING & RESTAURANTS

Notes

	TRIP # _____
🧭	FROM / TO
🗺️	ROUTE
⭕	MILEAGE

WEATHER CONDITIONS

🌡️ _____ ☀️ ⛅ 🌧️ ⛈️ ❄️

🚩 _____ ☐   ☐   ☐   ☐

📅 DATE

CAMPGROUND

	NAME		LOCATION	☆☆☆☆☆
	ADDRESS		SHOWERS	☆☆☆☆☆
	PHONE		CAMPSTORE	☆☆☆☆☆
	WEBSITE		LAUNDRY	☆☆☆☆☆
	SITE #		WATER PRESSURE	☆☆☆☆☆
	PRICE		OVERALL RATING	☆☆☆☆☆

HIGHLIGHTS

PLACES & ACTIVITIES

DINING & RESTAURANTS

Notes

TRIP # _____

- 🗺️ FROM / TO
- 🗺️ ROUTE
- 🚗 MILEAGE

WEATHER CONDITIONS

🌡️ _____   ☀️ ⛅ 🌧️ ⛈️ ❄️

🚩 _____   ☐ ☐ ☐ ☐ ☐

📅 DATE

CAMPGROUND

🏕️ NAME	🌲 LOCATION	☆☆☆☆☆
📍 ADDRESS	🚿 SHOWERS	☆☆☆☆☆
📞 PHONE	🏪 CAMPSTORE	☆☆☆☆☆
🌐 WEBSITE	🧺 LAUNDRY	☆☆☆☆☆
⛺ SITE #	🚰 WATER PRESSURE	☆☆☆☆☆
💵 PRICE	🤲 OVERALL RATING	☆☆☆☆☆

HIGHLIGHTS

PLACES & ACTIVITIES

DINING & RESTAURANTS

Notes

	TRIP # _____
🗺️	FROM / TO
🗺️	ROUTE
🚫	MILEAGE

WEATHER CONDITIONS					
🌡️ _____	☀️	⛅	🌧️	⛈️	❄️
🚩 _____	☐	☐	☐	☐	☐
📅 DATE					

CAMPGROUND

🏕️ NAME		🏞️ LOCATION		☆☆☆☆☆
📍 ADDRESS		🚿 SHOWERS		☆☆☆☆☆
📞 PHONE		🏪 CAMPSTORE		☆☆☆☆☆
🌐 WEBSITE		👕 LAUNDRY		☆☆☆☆☆
⛺ SITE #		🚰 WATER PRESSURE		☆☆☆☆☆
💵 PRICE		🙌 OVERALL RATING		☆☆☆☆☆

HIGHLIGHTS

_____
_____
_____
_____

PLACES & ACTIVITIES

_____
_____
_____
_____

DINING & RESTAURANTS

_____
_____
_____
_____

Notes

TRIP # _____		WEATHER CONDITIONS	
FROM / TO		🌡 _____ ☀ ⛅ 🌧 ⛈ ❄	
ROUTE		🚩 _____ ☐ ☐ ☐ ☐ ☐	
MILEAGE		DATE	

CAMPGROUND

NAME		LOCATION	☆☆☆☆☆
ADDRESS		SHOWERS	☆☆☆☆☆
PHONE		CAMPSTORE	☆☆☆☆☆
WEBSITE		LAUNDRY	☆☆☆☆☆
SITE #		WATER PRESSURE	☆☆☆☆☆
PRICE		OVERALL RATING	☆☆☆☆☆

HIGHLIGHTS

PLACES & ACTIVITIES

DINING & RESTAURANTS

Notes

	TRIP # _____
🗺	FROM / TO
🗺	ROUTE
⊘	MILEAGE

WEATHER CONDITIONS						
🌡 _____	☀	⛅	🌧	⛈	❄
🚩 _____	☐	☐	☐	☐	☐
📅 DATE					

CAMPGROUND

NAME		LOCATION	☆☆☆☆☆
ADDRESS		SHOWERS	☆☆☆☆☆
PHONE		CAMPSTORE	☆☆☆☆☆
WEBSITE		LAUNDRY	☆☆☆☆☆
SITE #		WATER PRESSURE	☆☆☆☆☆
PRICE		OVERALL RATING	☆☆☆☆☆

HIGHLIGHTS

PLACES & ACTIVITIES

DINING & RESTAURANTS

Notes

TRIP # _____

- FROM / TO
- ROUTE
- MILEAGE

WEATHER CONDITIONS

🌡 _____   ☀ ⛅ 🌧 ⛈ ❄
🚩 _____   ☐ ☐ ☐ ☐ ☐

📅 DATE

CAMPGROUND

NAME		LOCATION		☆☆☆☆☆
ADDRESS		SHOWERS		☆☆☆☆☆
PHONE		CAMPSTORE		☆☆☆☆☆
WEBSITE		LAUNDRY		☆☆☆☆☆
SITE #		WATER PRESSURE		☆☆☆☆☆
PRICE		OVERALL RATING		☆☆☆☆☆

HIGHLIGHTS

PLACES & ACTIVITIES

DINING & RESTAURANTS

Notes

	TRIP # _____
🗺️	FROM / TO
🗺️	ROUTE
⊘	MILEAGE

	WEATHER CONDITIONS
🌡️ _____	☀️ ⛅ 🌧️ ⛈️ ❄️
🚩 _____	☐ ☐ ☐ ☐ ☐
📅	DATE

CAMPGROUND

🏕️	NAME	🏞️	LOCATION	☆☆☆☆☆
📍	ADDRESS	🚿	SHOWERS	☆☆☆☆☆
📞	PHONE	🏪	CAMPSTORE	☆☆☆☆☆
🌐	WEBSITE	👕	LAUNDRY	☆☆☆☆☆
⛺	SITE #	🚰	WATER PRESSURE	☆☆☆☆☆
💵	PRICE	⭐	OVERALL RATING	☆☆☆☆☆

HIGHLIGHTS

PLACES & ACTIVITIES

DINING & RESTAURANTS

Notes

TRIP # ____

- FROM / TO
- ROUTE
- MILEAGE

WEATHER CONDITIONS

🌡 ____   ☀ ⛅ 🌧 ⛈ ❄
🚩 ____   ☐ ☐ ☐ ☐ ☐

📅 DATE

CAMPGROUND

NAME		LOCATION	☆☆☆☆☆
ADDRESS		SHOWERS	☆☆☆☆☆
PHONE		CAMPSTORE	☆☆☆☆☆
WEBSITE		LAUNDRY	☆☆☆☆☆
SITE #		WATER PRESSURE	☆☆☆☆☆
PRICE		OVERALL RATING	☆☆☆☆☆

HIGHLIGHTS

PLACES & ACTIVITIES

DINING & RESTAURANTS

Notes

	TRIP # _____
	FROM / TO
	ROUTE
	MILEAGE

WEATHER CONDITIONS		
🌡 _____	☀ 🌤 🌧 ⛈ ❄	
🚩 _____	☐ ☐ ☐ ☐ ☐	
📅 DATE		

CAMPGROUND

NAME		LOCATION	☆☆☆☆☆
ADDRESS		SHOWERS	☆☆☆☆☆
PHONE		CAMPSTORE	☆☆☆☆☆
WEBSITE		LAUNDRY	☆☆☆☆☆
SITE #		WATER PRESSURE	☆☆☆☆☆
PRICE		OVERALL RATING	☆☆☆☆☆

HIGHLIGHTS

PLACES & ACTIVITIES

DINING & RESTAURANTS

Notes

TRIP # _____

- FROM / TO
- ROUTE
- MILEAGE

WEATHER CONDITIONS

🌡 _____ ☀ ⛅ 🌧 ⛈ ❄
🚩 _____ ☐ ☐ ☐ ☐ ☐

📅 DATE

CAMPGROUND

NAME	LOCATION ☆☆☆☆☆
ADDRESS	SHOWERS ☆☆☆☆☆
PHONE	CAMPSTORE ☆☆☆☆☆
WEBSITE	LAUNDRY ☆☆☆☆☆
SITE #	WATER PRESSURE ☆☆☆☆☆
PRICE	OVERALL RATING ☆☆☆☆☆

HIGHLIGHTS

PLACES & ACTIVITIES

DINING & RESTAURANTS

Notes

TRIP # _____

- FROM / TO
- ROUTE
- MILEAGE

WEATHER CONDITIONS

🌡 _____ ☀️ ⛅ 🌧 ⛈ ❄️

🚩 _____ ☐ ☐ ☐ ☐ ☐

📅 DATE

CAMPGROUND

NAME	LOCATION	☆☆☆☆☆
ADDRESS	SHOWERS	☆☆☆☆☆
PHONE	CAMPSTORE	☆☆☆☆☆
WEBSITE	LAUNDRY	☆☆☆☆☆
SITE #	WATER PRESSURE	☆☆☆☆☆
PRICE	OVERALL RATING	☆☆☆☆☆

HIGHLIGHTS

PLACES & ACTIVITIES

DINING & RESTAURANTS

Notes

	TRIP # _____
🗺️	FROM / TO
🗺️	ROUTE
🧭	MILEAGE

	WEATHER CONDITIONS
🌡️ _____	☀️ ⛅ 🌧️ ⛈️ ❄️
🚩 _____	☐ ☐ ☐ ☐ ☐
📅	DATE

CAMPGROUND

🏕️	NAME	🏞️ LOCATION	☆☆☆☆☆
📍	ADDRESS	🚿 SHOWERS	☆☆☆☆☆
📞	PHONE	🏪 CAMPSTORE	☆☆☆☆☆
🌐	WEBSITE	👕 LAUNDRY	☆☆☆☆☆
⛺	SITE #	🚰 WATER PRESSURE	☆☆☆☆☆
💵	PRICE	🌟 OVERALL RATING	☆☆☆☆☆

HIGHLIGHTS

_____
_____
_____
_____

PLACES & ACTIVITIES

_____
_____
_____
_____
_____

DINING & RESTAURANTS

_____
_____
_____
_____
_____

Notes

	TRIP # _____
📍	FROM / TO
🗺️	ROUTE
🧭	MILEAGE

WEATHER CONDITIONS					
🌡️ _____	☀️	⛅	🌧️	⛈️	❄️
🚩 _____	☐	☐	☐	☐	☐
📅 DATE					

CAMPGROUND

🏕️ NAME		🌲 LOCATION		☆☆☆☆☆
📍 ADDRESS		🚿 SHOWERS		☆☆☆☆☆
📞 PHONE		🏪 CAMPSTORE		☆☆☆☆☆
🌐 WEBSITE		👕 LAUNDRY		☆☆☆☆☆
⛺ SITE #		🚰 WATER PRESSURE		☆☆☆☆☆
💵 PRICE		⭐ OVERALL RATING		☆☆☆☆☆

HIGHLIGHTS

PLACES & ACTIVITIES

DINING & RESTAURANTS

Notes

TRIP # _____	
FROM / TO	
ROUTE	
MILEAGE	

WEATHER CONDITIONS	
🌡 _____ ☀ ⛅ 🌧 ⛈ ❄	
🚩 _____ ☐ ☐ ☐ ☐ ☐	
DATE	

CAMPGROUND

NAME		LOCATION	☆☆☆☆☆
ADDRESS		SHOWERS	☆☆☆☆☆
PHONE		CAMPSTORE	☆☆☆☆☆
WEBSITE		LAUNDRY	☆☆☆☆☆
SITE #		WATER PRESSURE	☆☆☆☆☆
PRICE		OVERALL RATING	☆☆☆☆☆

HIGHLIGHTS

PLACES & ACTIVITIES

DINING & RESTAURANTS

Notes

TRIP # _____

- FROM / TO
- ROUTE
- MILEAGE

WEATHER CONDITIONS

🌡 _____ ☀️ ⛅ 🌧 ⛈ ❄️

🚩 _____ ☐ ☐ ☐ ☐ ☐

📅 DATE

CAMPGROUND

NAME	LOCATION	☆☆☆☆☆
ADDRESS	SHOWERS	☆☆☆☆☆
PHONE	CAMPSTORE	☆☆☆☆☆
WEBSITE	LAUNDRY	☆☆☆☆☆
SITE #	WATER PRESSURE	☆☆☆☆☆
PRICE	OVERALL RATING	☆☆☆☆☆

HIGHLIGHTS

PLACES & ACTIVITIES

DINING & RESTAURANTS

Notes

TRIP # _____

- FROM / TO
- ROUTE
- MILEAGE

WEATHER CONDITIONS

🌡 _____ ☀️ ⛅ 🌧 ⛈ ❄️
🚩 _____ ☐ ☐ ☐ ☐ ☐

📅 DATE

CAMPGROUND

NAME	LOCATION	☆☆☆☆☆
ADDRESS	SHOWERS	☆☆☆☆☆
PHONE	CAMPSTORE	☆☆☆☆☆
WEBSITE	LAUNDRY	☆☆☆☆☆
SITE #	WATER PRESSURE	☆☆☆☆☆
PRICE	OVERALL RATING	☆☆☆☆☆

HIGHLIGHTS

PLACES & ACTIVITIES

DINING & RESTAURANTS

Notes

TRIP # _____		WEATHER CONDITIONS	
🗺️ FROM / TO		🌡️ _____ ☀️ ⛅ 🌧️ ⛈️ ❄️	
🗺️ ROUTE		🚩 _____ ☐ ☐ ☐ ☐ ☐	
⭕ MILEAGE		📅 DATE	

CAMPGROUND

NAME		LOCATION	☆☆☆☆☆
ADDRESS		SHOWERS	☆☆☆☆☆
PHONE		CAMPSTORE	☆☆☆☆☆
WEBSITE		LAUNDRY	☆☆☆☆☆
SITE #		WATER PRESSURE	☆☆☆☆☆
PRICE		OVERALL RATING	☆☆☆☆☆

HIGHLIGHTS

PLACES & ACTIVITIES

DINING & RESTAURANTS

Notes

TRIP # _____

- FROM / TO
- ROUTE
- MILEAGE

WEATHER CONDITIONS

🌡 _____ ☀ ⛅ 🌧 ⛈ ❄

🚩 _____ ☐ ☐ ☐ ☐ ☐

📅 DATE

CAMPGROUND

NAME	LOCATION ☆☆☆☆☆
ADDRESS	SHOWERS ☆☆☆☆☆
PHONE	CAMPSTORE ☆☆☆☆☆
WEBSITE	LAUNDRY ☆☆☆☆☆
SITE #	WATER PRESSURE ☆☆☆☆☆
PRICE	OVERALL RATING ☆☆☆☆☆

HIGHLIGHTS

PLACES & ACTIVITIES

DINING & RESTAURANTS

Notes

TRIP # _____		WEATHER CONDITIONS	
🗺️ FROM / TO		🌡️ _____ ☀️ ⛅ 🌧️ ⛈️ ❄️	
🗺️ ROUTE		🚩 _____ ☐ ☐ ☐ ☐ ☐	
⭕ MILEAGE		📅 DATE	

CAMPGROUND

🏕️ NAME		🌲 LOCATION	☆☆☆☆☆
📍 ADDRESS		🚿 SHOWERS	☆☆☆☆☆
📞 PHONE		🏪 CAMPSTORE	☆☆☆☆☆
🌐 WEBSITE		👕 LAUNDRY	☆☆☆☆☆
⛺ SITE #		🚰 WATER PRESSURE	☆☆☆☆☆
💵 PRICE		⭐ OVERALL RATING	☆☆☆☆☆

HIGHLIGHTS

PLACES & ACTIVITIES	DINING & RESTAURANTS

Notes

TRIP # _____

- FROM / TO
- ROUTE
- MILEAGE

WEATHER CONDITIONS

🌡 _____   ☀ ⛅ 🌧 ⛈ ❄

🏳 _____   ☐ ☐ ☐ ☐ ☐

- DATE

CAMPGROUND

NAME		LOCATION	☆☆☆☆☆
ADDRESS		SHOWERS	☆☆☆☆☆
PHONE		CAMPSTORE	☆☆☆☆☆
WEBSITE		LAUNDRY	☆☆☆☆☆
SITE #		WATER PRESSURE	☆☆☆☆☆
PRICE		OVERALL RATING	☆☆☆☆☆

HIGHLIGHTS

PLACES & ACTIVITIES

DINING & RESTAURANTS

Notes

TRIP # _____		WEATHER CONDITIONS	
FROM / TO		🌡 _____ ☀ ⛅ 🌧 ⛈ ❄	
ROUTE		🚩 _____ ☐ ☐ ☐ ☐ ☐	
MILEAGE		DATE	

CAMPGROUND

NAME		LOCATION	☆☆☆☆☆
ADDRESS		SHOWERS	☆☆☆☆☆
PHONE		CAMPSTORE	☆☆☆☆☆
WEBSITE		LAUNDRY	☆☆☆☆☆
SITE #		WATER PRESSURE	☆☆☆☆☆
PRICE		OVERALL RATING	☆☆☆☆☆

HIGHLIGHTS

PLACES & ACTIVITIES

DINING & RESTAURANTS

Notes

	TRIP # _____
FROM / TO	
ROUTE	
MILEAGE	

WEATHER CONDITIONS

🌡 _____ ☀ ⛅ 🌧 ⛈ ❄
🚩 _____ ☐ ☐ ☐ ☐ ☐

📅 DATE

CAMPGROUND

NAME		LOCATION	☆☆☆☆☆
ADDRESS		SHOWERS	☆☆☆☆☆
PHONE		CAMPSTORE	☆☆☆☆☆
WEBSITE		LAUNDRY	☆☆☆☆☆
SITE #		WATER PRESSURE	☆☆☆☆☆
PRICE		OVERALL RATING	☆☆☆☆☆

HIGHLIGHTS

PLACES & ACTIVITIES

DINING & RESTAURANTS

Notes

TRIP # _____

- FROM / TO
- ROUTE
- MILEAGE

WEATHER CONDITIONS

- 🌡 _____ ☀ ⛅ 🌦 🌧 ❄
- 🚩 _____ ☐ ☐ ☐ ☐ ☐
- DATE

CAMPGROUND

NAME	LOCATION	☆☆☆☆☆
ADDRESS	SHOWERS	☆☆☆☆☆
PHONE	CAMPSTORE	☆☆☆☆☆
WEBSITE	LAUNDRY	☆☆☆☆☆
SITE #	WATER PRESSURE	☆☆☆☆☆
PRICE	OVERALL RATING	☆☆☆☆☆

HIGHLIGHTS

PLACES & ACTIVITIES

DINING & RESTAURANTS

Notes

TRIP # _____	
FROM / TO	
ROUTE	
MILEAGE	

WEATHER CONDITIONS

🌡 _____ ☀️ ⛅ 🌧 ⛈ ❄️
🚩 _____   ☐   ☐   ☐   ☐   ☐

📅 DATE

CAMPGROUND

NAME		LOCATION	☆☆☆☆☆
ADDRESS		SHOWERS	☆☆☆☆☆
PHONE		CAMPSTORE	☆☆☆☆☆
WEBSITE		LAUNDRY	☆☆☆☆☆
SITE #		WATER PRESSURE	☆☆☆☆☆
PRICE		OVERALL RATING	☆☆☆☆☆

HIGHLIGHTS

PLACES & ACTIVITIES

DINING & RESTAURANTS

Notes

TRIP # _____

- FROM / TO
- ROUTE
- MILEAGE

WEATHER CONDITIONS

☀️ ⛅ 🌧️ ⛈️ ❄️
☐ ☐ ☐ ☐ ☐

DATE

CAMPGROUND

NAME	LOCATION	☆☆☆☆☆
ADDRESS	SHOWERS	☆☆☆☆☆
PHONE	CAMPSTORE	☆☆☆☆☆
WEBSITE	LAUNDRY	☆☆☆☆☆
SITE #	WATER PRESSURE	☆☆☆☆☆
PRICE	OVERALL RATING	☆☆☆☆☆

HIGHLIGHTS

PLACES & ACTIVITIES

DINING & RESTAURANTS

Notes

TRIP # _____

- FROM / TO
- ROUTE
- MILEAGE

WEATHER CONDITIONS

🌡 _____ ☀️ ⛅ 🌧 ⛈ ❄️
🚩 _____ ☐ ☐ ☐ ☐ ☐

📅 DATE

CAMPGROUND

NAME	LOCATION	☆☆☆☆☆
ADDRESS	SHOWERS	☆☆☆☆☆
PHONE	CAMPSTORE	☆☆☆☆☆
WEBSITE	LAUNDRY	☆☆☆☆☆
SITE #	WATER PRESSURE	☆☆☆☆☆
PRICE	OVERALL RATING	☆☆☆☆☆

HIGHLIGHTS

PLACES & ACTIVITIES

DINING & RESTAURANTS

Notes

	TRIP # _____
📍	FROM / TO
🗺️	ROUTE
🚗	MILEAGE

WEATHER CONDITIONS					
🌡️ _____	☀️	⛅	🌧️	⛈️	❄️
🚩 _____	☐	☐	☐	☐	☐
📅 DATE					

CAMPGROUND

NAME		LOCATION	☆☆☆☆☆
ADDRESS		SHOWERS	☆☆☆☆☆
PHONE		CAMPSTORE	☆☆☆☆☆
WEBSITE		LAUNDRY	☆☆☆☆☆
SITE #		WATER PRESSURE	☆☆☆☆☆
PRICE		OVERALL RATING	☆☆☆☆☆

HIGHLIGHTS

_____
_____
_____
_____

PLACES & ACTIVITIES	DINING & RESTAURANTS

Notes

Printed in Great Britain
by Amazon